This Means Stop

by **Myka-Lynne Sokoloff**
illustrated by **Larry Paulsen**

Scott Foresman

Editorial Offices: Glenview, Illinois • New York, New York
Sales Offices: Reading, Massachusetts • Duluth, Georgia
Glenview, Illinois • Carrollton, Texas • Menlo Park, California

Who can stop now?
We can stop now.

Who can go now?
They can go now.

Who can turn now?
They can turn now.

Who can go so slow?

They can go so slow.

Now we can go.

Who says so?

She says so.
Go!